插图珍藏版

By Samuel Taylor Coleridge

The Rime of the Ancient Mariner

[英]塞缪尔·泰勒·柯勒律治 著 [美]爱德华·A·威尔逊 绘

叶紫 译

江苏凤凰文艺出版社

图书在版编目（CIP）数据

古舟子咏：插图珍藏版/（英）塞缪尔·泰勒·柯勒律治著；（美）爱德华·A·威尔逊绘；叶紫译.--南京：江苏凤凰文艺出版社，2022.12

ISBN 978-7-5594-6518-4

Ⅰ.①古… Ⅱ.①塞…②爱…③叶… Ⅲ.①诗歌-英国-近代 Ⅳ.① I561.24

中国版本图书馆 CIP 数据核字 (2022) 第 159408 号

古舟子咏（插图珍藏版）

[英] 塞缪尔·泰勒·柯勒律治 著　　[美] 爱德华·A·威尔逊 绘　　叶紫 译

策　　划	尚　飞
责任编辑	曹　波
特约编辑	毛菊丹
装帧设计	墨白空间·陈威伸
出版发行	江苏凤凰文艺出版社
	南京市中央路 165 号，邮编：210009
网　　址	http://www.jswenyi.com
印　　刷	天津图文方嘉印刷有限公司
开　　本	889 毫米 ×1194 毫米　1/16
印　　张	7.75
字　　数	30 千字
版　　次	2022 年 12 月第 1 版
印　　次	2022 年 12 月第 1 次印刷
书　　号	ISBN 978-7-5594-6518-4
定　　价	88.00 元

江苏凤凰文艺版图书凡印刷、装订错误，可向出版社调换，联系电话 025-83280257

寒冰举起高樯，从旁漂过，
绿如翡翠一般

序　言[1]

1

发现自己被卷入无法解释或无法相信的境地时，每一个凡人都会本能地寻求某种根植深处的东西，来保持对现实的稳固把握。这便是《古舟子咏》的读者所面临的困境。诚然，呈现在读者眼前的，是明确而可感的事实：连绵不绝的天空，路线清晰的航程。但那又大又亮又圆的太阳蒙上道道肋影；死者复活，冰冷的眼眸映出闪闪月辉；暗淡的群星起舞夜幕，织出一派异象。最原始的天空本身，与大海一起，被海天间的鬼灵精怪触碰，染上怪诞的色调。可尽管如此，柯勒律治的敏锐直觉从未出错。无论诗中的场景如何转化，船的航行轨道又如何随之延伸，都有另一条活动的准则贯穿始终，它就像一连串永恒的山丘，起伏在诡异的光影变幻之下：它是人类古老而传统的信念之一。它构成了《古舟子咏》最引人注目的形式要素。

《古舟子咏》前六个部分的部末诗节分别标志着情节演化的六个阶段。让我们将这六个诗节中最值得注意的词句暂时抽离语境：

【第一部分】　……我用十字弓

---

[1] 该序言原为美国著名学者、批评家、柯勒律治研究专家约翰·利文斯顿·洛斯（John Livingston Lowes，1867—1945）的著作《上都之路》（*The Road to Xanadu*）中的第十六章。——后文中未标明原注者均为译注。

<u>射死了信天翁。</u>[1]

这便是一切的开端。

【第二部分】　他们把<u>死鸟</u>当作十字，
　　　　　　<u>挂在我的颈间</u>。

重重后果开始找上破坏者。

【第三部分】　（五十有四，两百个活人……
　　　　　　一个一个倒地。）
　　　　　　<u>每一个灵魂都像弩箭嗖嗖</u>，
　　　　　　<u>从我身边掠过！</u>

后果延伸到破坏者之外，落向同船的人。然后，"'死中之生'开始把老水手耍弄"[2]，直到情节出现转折：

多么快乐的生灵！美得
没有言语能描述：
爱的甘泉从心底涌起，
不觉间，我送上了祝福，
准是慈悲的天神垂怜于我，

接着：

【第四部分】　那一刻，我终于能开口祷告；

---

[1] 诗文截取部分中，序言的作者在原文中用斜体加以强调的部分用下划直线标出。
[2] 序言中的直接引用用下划波浪线标出，后同。

脖子又能自由转动,
<u>信天翁掉落,像铅一样</u>
<u>直直坠入海中。</u>

破坏行为招致的沉重负担就此掉落,但破坏行为的结果不留情面,持续发酵。

【第五部分】 另一个声音更加温柔,
似汩汩蜜露:
他说:"此人已受到惩罚,
<u>惩罚还没有结束</u>。"

但至少航程有其注定的终点,隐士的出场鸣响了有别于之前的音符。

【第六部分】 <u>他将洗净信天翁的血迹</u>,
赦免我灵魂的罪恶。

可连宽恕也——两次——离他而去:离"行为的造物"(the deed's creature)而去。

【第七部分】 此后,那痛苦去了又来,
不定在哪个时候:
这吓人的故事从头讲完,
我心头的烈火方休。

<u>我像夜晚一样四处流浪</u>,
我的言语有奇怪的力量,
在遇见某人的那一刹那,

> 我便知道他要听我说话，
> 他就是我讲述的对象。

因果之链没有穷尽。老水手回到故国的港湾，灵魂被赦免，"一生之罚"随一行短注的出现而"降下"，为诗歌情节（虽非诗歌本身）画上句点。

以上，便是《古舟子咏》的草图，它被富于谋略的诗节布置揭示并强烈地凸显出来。一位建筑大师绘制并完成了它。船的航程划下贯穿全图的宏大结构线；同样影响了情节发展的种种精灵、幽灵式的形体和天使——像那些沿着轨道，与彗星同步的"智思之灵"(Intellectual Spirits) 一样——以均匀的速度随船而动，循线而前。三条不断成形的主线[1]各有其独立的演化方式，但每一条主线的发展又与另外两条紧密相扣。各大基本要素互相渗透，保持协调，让《古舟子咏》成为一个高度统一的整体；这种渗透与协调源于创构性的想象，成于精湛绝顶的建造技艺，是最高明的艺术家才能实现的成就。谈及他在伦敦基督慈幼学校念书时的老师詹姆斯·博伊尔 (James Boyer) 时，柯勒律治说："我从他那里学到，诗歌，包括最崇高的诗篇在内，自有其独特的、像科学逻辑一样严密的逻辑，连最狂野的颂歌似乎也是这样；而且，诗的逻辑比科学逻辑更难把握，因为它更加微妙、复杂，更具依赖性，也有更难以捉摸的动因。"《古舟子咏》的逻辑便是如此。

2

对《古舟子咏》而言，因果链条的存在并不仅仅是为了巩固逻辑。它就是人生，就是每一个人所了解的人生。你做下一件傻事、恶事，

---

[1] 三条主线即"因果的链条""航海的线路"与"精灵的作用"。

种种后果便不仅像回家一样寻你而来，也足具寻他人而去的倾向。你忏悔，一副重担便被提离，不再压抑你的灵魂。可你并未因此而摆脱你的作为。你取得原谅，可因果规律无动于衷，不断生效；愚行、恶行虽经忏悔，但其重重后果仍将继续收割你的余生，直到最后一刻。这并非某种道德体系，而是不可更易的人生法则。它就在那里，主导着所有人生经验，不因你我而异。对它，我们"了解、熟悉"——如果世上真的存在能被"了解、熟悉"的东西。

艺术的效用起于错觉 (illusion)——"那种诗意的、艺术性的"，一如爱弥儿 (Amiel) 所言，"不以和现实本身混为一体为目标的错觉。"但"真实"又必须以某种方式构成它的"根基"，否则，错觉的魔咒便难以持续。柯勒律治已经直截了当地表明他想通过《古舟子咏》来达成的目标，即："从内在天性中调动一份人性的关注和某种真实的假象，来确保（这些）想象的影子能在构成'诗性信念'(poetic faith) 的那一瞬间获得那份心甘情愿的'怀疑暂停'(suspension of disbelief)。"阅读《古舟子咏》时，正如约翰·德莱顿[1]谈及赏戏经历时所言，"我们知道自己会被欺骗，也希望如此。"但我们又只会在错觉以某种形式披上真实的假象之际接受错觉。和《古舟子咏》的所有活体纤维息息相关，堪称全诗骨肉之骨肉的，是一种和该隐的故事一样古老，又和昨天的经历一样新鲜的真实。读诗之际，我们会不自觉地说出"是的，这里——这便是人生——还有这里——这里"，仿佛在一片云雾缭绕的梦幻壮景中，我们连连瞥见了熟悉的山丘，那依稀可辨的轮廓时时显现，令人心安，而怀疑——那份已然在极地冰界与热带海境的生动现实面前产生动摇的怀疑——也被我们心甘情愿地暂停，没入那短暂的、独属于《古舟子咏》的诗之瞬间：这便是诗人的唯一期望。

于是，以老水手射杀信天翁为开端的情节序列便成功发挥出两大功效：它统一并（再次借用柯勒律治自撰的术语来说）"可信

---

[1] 约翰·德莱顿（John Dryden，1630—1700），英国诗人、剧作家、批评家。

化"(crediblize)了《古舟子咏》。它还有第三大功效吗？也就是说，它可有教化之效？对于柯勒律治的说教倾向，我心知肚明。然而，将《古舟子咏》的要旨解读成有意为之的道德教训，不仅会让柯勒律治，也会让作此解读的人显得愚笨而荒唐。这样的解读会彻底摧毁那个成为《古舟子咏》的真正本质的错觉世界：

> 美丽的世界
> 被你用强劲的
> 拳头摧毁，
> 在倾塌、在崩溃！[1]

柯勒律治无心教导种瓜得瓜种豆得豆的道理（尽管对此真理他深信不疑）。他要做的，是在想象出一个世界之后赋予它梦幻般的构造以连贯性与内在的一致性。这个世界既已存在（如果它不曾存在，便不会有诗；如果它以另一种方式存在，便不会有这一首诗），那么它不容侵犯的一致性便是我们在"那一瞬间"接受其有效性与可信性的唯一条件。柯勒律治凭借卓越的诗艺让《古舟子咏》达到了要求。

然而，这一不可或缺的条件的满足会带来一个同样不可避免的结果：要实现能创造出"现实错觉"的内在一贯性，就必须牺牲进入错觉领域的各式元素的完整性。这些元素，一如诗人自己的本性，也会"像染工的手一样被沉抑在其职责所在"。经过悉心打造，这些元素将与彼此，也与整体达成一致，染上梦幻世界的色彩，而一旦染上这般色彩，那么色彩有多浓厚，它们便在多大程度上丧失了原本的独立性，脱离了一个独立的存在所特有的状态。诗歌的力量再强，也无法在变换现实的同时保有纯粹而本真的现实性。在这些

1　语出歌德《浮士德》。

元素和《古舟子咏》的肌理完全融合之后，逐步发展并贯穿全诗的一系列经验性真实都将失去所有说教价值，任何寄寓诗中的道德教诲也将失效。

毕竟，处于《古舟子咏》之外的"道德"站不住脚。不在那"魔环"之内，它就不会生效。船从赤道向南，驶入极地，绕过好望角后，再北归赤道，画下一个完全有现实可能的大圈。但精灵、幽魂、天使和返生的亡魂接连出没，时隐时现，老水手的航程虽有可能是真实航程的华丽变形，却也很难被视作一份介绍赤道海域和极地海域的动物生态的实用指南。残酷的因果主线随着航程的延续而延续，与航程本身一样坚定，直到全诗结束。可如果从现实世界的角度来看，诗中的因果可谓前后失调，实在荒谬。老水手射杀一只海鸟，竟有水中灵怪协同鬼船一艘，前来向他寻仇；出于一股爱的冲动，他祝福了海中生灵，竟唤得一群天使从天而降，来为无人驾驶的大船领航。而且，只因老水手射死了一只海鸟，两百个水手倒地而亡，凶手本人也注定要踏上没有终点的赎罪之路。用一个罪罚平衡的世界的标准来衡量，如此"量刑"显然与弑鸟之罪不相匹配。然而，《古舟子咏》的情节赖以发展的世界——那个既已存在的世界——并非一个罪罚平衡的球形世界。在那个鸟有精灵守护，船有幽灵、天使之力推动的世界里，这样的后果与前因始终协调（如果在"那一瞬间"，我们接受诗人设下的前提），而《古舟子咏》的道德背景则被柯勒律治用来营造一种错觉：那种非同一般的不合理性好像存乎必然。为人熟知的道德价值，连同那条为人熟知的航线轮廓，在柯勒律治笔下得到了极富想象力的运用。在这一点上，《古舟子咏》和旨在宣传教化性道德条款的虚构故事相去千里。

关于这一点，可以说，柯勒律治自己就已作出了相当明确的澄清，我之所以费此周章，重复予以说明，正是因为"本诗无关说教"这一基本原则一直不断地遭到曲解。比如，一位杰出的现代批评家从勃朗宁¹的某些诗文中得出"走出门外，让自我与风景混为一体，是人之本分"这一推论之后，又继续写道："作为一种救赎方法，这比老水手的方法还更容易，且更具美感。人们怎会忘记，他竟要通过赞美海蛇的色彩来摆脱罪孽的重担！"这种说法自是在泛灵空想公正而严苛的质询之下提出了"一种无痛无苦，可以替代真正的精神努力的方法"，但作为一种有关柯勒律治如何诗以言教的解读，它必须被严肃对待，尽管它不无某种辛辣的逗趣之感。事实上，老水手对海蛇的赞美²并非诗中那些直白的语句所宣称的那种救赎（幸与白璧德³教授的假定不谋而合），但这一点无关紧要。这份批评的真正价值在于，它揭示出，当我们忽视一件艺术作品的根本前提，并像解读一份单纯的道德文献一样解读它时，会发生什么。照这样解读，再往下推断，便会得出合理的结论：柯勒律治拥护"老水手杀了一只海鸟，所以全船船员被残忍屠杀"这一因果连环在道德上的适切性，《古舟子咏》这份道德文献有多纯粹，柯勒律治的拥护便有多严肃。——这无疑是在归谬其他所有可能。的确，柯勒律治曾频繁抛开诗人的身份，而且，很有可能，在不做诗人的时候，他也会流露出对"泛灵空想"(pantheistic revery)的痴迷。但在创作《古舟子咏》时，他对诗文的建构始终遵循明确的准则，他保持着再清醒不过的意识，知道自己正写下一部"纯属想象"的作品。我所引用的这份批评的谬误之处就在于，它绕过了《古舟子咏》的基本假定——"那种诗意的、艺术性的，不以和现实本身混为一体为目标的错觉。"

关于《古舟子咏》的"道德问题"，柯勒律治本人也不无说法。在《文学传记》(*Biographia Literaria*) 中出现明确声明十五年后，

---

1 罗伯特·勃朗宁（Robert Browning，1812—1889），英国诗人、剧作家。
2 见全诗第四部分第十四诗节。
3 欧文·白璧德（Irving Babbitt，1865—1933），美国文学批评家、人文主义者，在思想上重视伦理道德，反对浪漫主义。

全诗著毕三十二年之后，他在谈话中忆及《古舟子咏》：

> 巴勃尔德[1]夫人曾对我说，她非常欣赏《古舟子咏》，但诗中有两个错误，一是它不太可信，二是它没有道德[2]。要说可不可信，我承认，这或许是个问题；可至于道德的缺失，我对她说，依我自己的判断，诗里的道德已经太多，而《古舟子咏》的唯一错误，或者说，它的首要错误，如果可以这么说的话，就在于，在一部如此纯粹的想象之作里，一份道德情操，作为某种原则或动因，被如此无所顾忌地强加给读者。它不该有那么多道德，就该像《天方夜谭》里的那则故事一样：商人坐在井边吃枣，边吃边把枣壳扔到一旁；忽然！一个妖怪出现，说他必须杀掉这个商人，因为他扔掉的一块枣壳好像弄瞎了妖怪儿子的眼睛。

言下之意明确无疑。柯勒律治（觉得自己）出于安全考量，可能过分掩盖了《古舟子咏》的前提：毕竟，那是"巴勃尔德夫人们"的世界，她们汲汲于道德，无教而不诗，一如其汲汲于面包黄油，少之而茶废；《古舟子咏》中的道德情操如此显见，她们必定会伸手进去，欣然掏出自己的诗意——事实上也是如此。"在一部如此纯粹的想象之作里，一份道德情操，作为某种原则或动因，被如此无所顾忌地强加给读者。"——说到这里，柯勒律治暂作停顿。在

---

1 安娜·巴勃尔德（Anna Barbauld，1743—1825），英国诗人、散文家、儿童文学作家。
2 查尔斯·兰姆（Charles Lamb，1775—1834，英国散文家）有过一次光芒万丈的、能充分阐明巴勃尔德夫人其人及其批评的"火山式喷发"。1802年10月，在给柯勒律治的信中，兰姆写道："很高兴鼻烟和给 Pi-pos（译者按：Pi-pos 即柯勒律治之子德文特·柯勒律治）的书令你们满意。《古迪两只鞋》(*Goody Two-Shoes*) 几乎已经绝版。巴勃尔德夫人的大作已经驱逐了所有童话童谣中的古老经典……巴夫人书里那些无关紧要、了无生气的知识好像成了小孩子在知识形成的过程中不得不接收的东西；光学了'马'是一种动物，'山羊'比'马'更好之类的玩意，就得昂起空空的脑袋，摆出一副知识就是力量的架势；他们根本读不到那些充满野性的故事，接触不到那种能让孩子长大成人的美丽'志趣'，还一个劲儿地怀疑自己是不是个长不大的孩子……去他的！——我骂的就是巴勃尔德那一群人，真是可恨至极！'人'性的一切，大人的也好，小孩的也好，全都蔫了、萎了。"——原注

他看来，《古舟子咏》的"唯一错误，或者说，它的首要错误"，是一个技术性错误。他并未着力确保那一瞬间的怀疑暂停，反倒不顾风险，坚定地植入了一种信念！其实，柯勒律治无需惧怕历史名人"巴勃尔德夫人"的道德指摘，因为对她来说，即便是在老水手于诗末告别时所表现出来的那份虔诚——那份在我看来恐怕足以让柯勒律治（和我们）感到遗憾[1]的虔诚之中，道德情操的强加也还不够无所顾忌。如果老水手杀的，不是一只海鸟，而是同船的某一个人，她或许才能理解——但这样一来，《古舟子咏》便不会存在。

引发一连串惊人后果的起因之"小"，正是《古舟子咏》意欲传达的印象能得以传达的先决条件。对全诗的构思而言，起因与后果的量级差异必不可少。试想，假如被害者不是海鸟，而是某一个人，你会有怎样的印象（在上一段话里，我就已略有暗示）？除此之外，我的确不知还有哪条捷径能让我们立刻领略到《古舟子咏》的独特艺术。一则（正如柯勒律治所感受到的那样）与《天方夜谭》中的不朽奇谭血脉相通，并因此而获得了不可剥夺的魔力的故事满受激发，饱汲活力，变成一幅怪诞难解的悲剧漫画。一片鸟羽落下，故事泉涌而出，以音乐为石，建成一座空中穹宫，而拱顶与支柱的倒影却漂然浪中[2]。它赖以形成的世界，在本质上，是一场幻梦的世界。梦与现实越不相称，故事的情节就越不合理；阅读之际，在一场艺术奇迹的影响下，我们被某种隐秘而亲切的逻辑张力深深迷住；那种连续不断、无可抗拒，比现实还更真实的逻辑感，正是这场幻梦最摄人心魄的错觉。"没有必然关联的事件并不互为因果"，华兹华斯在他针对《古舟子咏》的惨酷苛评中有此怨言。的确，梦

---

1 写到这里，我再次欣然借助于查尔斯·兰姆，这一回，他抗议的，是罗伯特·骚塞（Robert Southey，1774—1843，英国诗人）："道德应该在诗人的打造下融入一首诗的身体与灵魂、实质与趋向，而不是像提货单上最后那句'上帝保佑好船入港'一样被标在诗尾。"——原注

2 本句中的"泉涌""音乐""穹宫"和"倒影"均与柯勒律治的另一首名作《忽必烈汗》（*Kubla Khan*）有关。

里的事件不会互相引发，但它们似乎可以。这便是《古舟子咏》的情节得以发展的唯一条件。

"吸引我吧，我便快跑相随，"《雅歌》中的少女喊道，"我长得虽黑，却很秀美。"对错觉的接受便是错觉的凭据。"对我来说，"查尔斯·兰姆在写给华兹华斯的信中说道，"人类的故事里没有任何一则曾让我如此感动。第一遍读完，我就被彻底迷住，且一迷多日——里面那些不可思议的东西，我都不喜欢，可那海天变幻之下，那水手的种种情感却像童谣里风笛手汤姆的魔音一样，拽着我读到最后。"就在兰姆的话（而非我等基于批判研究而作出的判定）中，隐藏着《古舟子咏》的根本特性。可以说，兰姆的证词不仅道出了千万后世读者的心声，也就《古舟子咏》的错觉艺术——和"道德"艺术！——作出了定论。

3

我们试图理解的，是想象的运作方式。现在，《古舟子咏》的三股宏大的主线清晰地展现在眼前，让我们稍作停顿，确定自己所处的位置。我们踏上长途冒险之路，正穿越一片变幻莫测的地域，似乎到处都是意识与无意识的碰撞、偶然与非偶然的矛盾，我们能找到一个坚实的立足点吗？像《古舟子咏》这样一首梦幻之诗是否仅仅是潜意识活动的最终成果和无数休眠意象的汇集？或者，它是否完全是某种创构性能量——某种源源不绝，有其明确的意图，为了达成目的而全凭自身的意志从记忆中尽取所需、重拾万千意象，并有意识地用种种微妙的方式加以融合的创构性能量——的产物？还有，那种表面上的不协调是否有其调和之道？

《古舟子咏》的背后挤满了丰富多样到难以想象的意象。这一点毫无疑问。可《古舟子咏》并非这些意象的总合，一如无数闪闪发亮的金刚石微粒被拢成一堆，并不构成一颗钻石；同样，柯勒律治也不仅仅是个敏感化的媒介，只为接受并传递这些意象而在。此外，在诗文之下，在有意识的心理层面之下，这些意象更经历过难以次计的交混与融合。这一点也已没有争议。可《古舟子咏》亦非在无意识中交相混融的意象的汇合，一如零散的水滴合在一起，并不构成一池清水；同样，柯勒律治也绝非某个潜意识世界里的梦游者。构成《古舟子咏》的，既非有意识的意象，也非无意识的穿插渗透。二者都是不可分割的成分，可单凭这两种成分，无法创造出这样一个独立的实体。相反，从强劲有力的"源泉"之水里升腾而起的每一种意象、每一个崭新的造物，都已通过参与到一个整体之中来获得其现有的状态与特质。那是一个在方方面面都已作为一个整体被预见到的整体——塑造并成就它的，是一种长于掌控、富于想象的构思。《古舟子咏》独一无二、不可言喻的本质——正是它的形式[1]（form）。

这一诗歌形式源自精于选择的手艺，出自善于引导的智思，成于艰苦卓绝的脑力劳动[2]。起初，呈现在柯勒律治心中的，并不是一番固定在透明晶体中的景致，《古舟子咏》的整体构思既不清晰，也不完整。诗人心中混杂着无数形态各异的偶然暗示，这份构思只是一番潜在的景致，与上百种来回盘旋的替代方案同在。要像"直辟罗马大道"一样从那一片混杂中牵出作为结构主线的清晰航线，

---

[1] 此处所说的"形式"包含韵律模式、诗行长短、分节方式、情节安排等诸多方面。

[2] 柯勒律治在1800年的一封信中谈到《克里斯塔贝尔》（*Christabel*）时说："每写一行，我都得经受一阵分娩之痛。"此外，在一张写给罗伯特·骚塞，随1817年版《俗世布道》（*Lay Sermon*）的稿件一起被保存下来的便笺上，柯勒律治又说："一想起光是为了避免或修复那些一万个人里不会有一个人注意到的瑕疵，就费了多少精力，我便头晕目眩，恶心想吐。"华兹华斯也曾对柯勒律治的侄孙约翰·柯勒律治大法官说："专注于一种新韵律实验（译者按：《古舟子咏》大体由四行式民谣诗节构成；基本上，每个诗节里，第一、三行为抑扬四步诗行，每行包含四声重音，第二、四行为抑扬三步诗行，每行包含三声重音，大致遵循短行押韵原则；同时，柯勒律治通过额外音节的添加和额外诗行的插入等手法丰富了节奏，强化了音乐表现力；中文译文亦力图保留并重现了诗文的韵律）时，他（柯勒律治）所投入的时间与精力是难以想象的。"诚然，作品比诗人本身更有说服力，但这样的证词也无一多余。它们的存在更令我们深信，在一部纯属想象的诗作的构建过程中，分娩的阵痛和闪过脑海的幻景一样，都扮演着重要的角色。——原注

保持对立平衡的精灵之力与天使之力，和起于初始行为、不断发展延续的后果序列——需要的不仅仅是隐秘意象的自发进涌。无疑，那些像空中飞船一样连连闪过柯勒律治勤于孕育的脑海，一刻也不消停的迅捷联想从一开始就在产生效用，提供协助。这并不是在暗示，柯勒律治在（或者大约在）1797年10月13日从自我的整体中抽身，置身一块"冷静的颅盖"之下，在干冷的光线中酝酿他的计划，然后才打开了一扇扇通往各式禀赋的大门，从静默中唤醒了沉睡的意象。无论是在《古舟子咏》成形之初，还是在它"不断生长"之际，柯勒律治的所有才智，不管有无意识，都不动则已，一动俱动。这份研究[1]中的每一页文字几乎都以直接或间接的方式揭示出了创造性力量不顾意志的命令，自行运作生效时留下的痕迹；我最不愿意做的，就是在研究中低估这种模糊不明却充满力量的影响力。然而，让《古舟子咏》成为诗歌——而非明亮意象的聚集体——的能量，正是人类大脑通过思考来厘清混乱，并凭借居于脑后、驱策一切的意志的纯粹力量来治理乱局，为之注入明确的整体秩序的能力。成群的意象发光发亮，在潜意识层面互相融合，但那不可抗拒的构思之力却始终"像如主临奴的白昼"一样雄踞其上。作为组成部分的意象无论源于何处，都已在打磨之下，完美融入了建构全诗的思想所设定的场景。各式联想完成惊人的汇聚，透印出巨大的船影，在影中孕育光芒耀眼的海洋生物，在对称光影的同时，将这正因对称才得其平衡之美的画面锁入诗歌的基本架构。在令人窒息的那一瞬间，红日落海，群星奔涌，暗夜霎时降临——当各式元素纷然出现在景中，引发混乱，这一壮丽的"聚点"足具存在的理由：不是为其本身而存在，而是为了让夜幕的沉降与鬼船的消失同时获得不可思议的速度。血红的太阳正对桅顶，高悬在铜黄、炙热的天空，也不是为它自身而悬，而是为了在掌控着诗文发展方向的航线

---

[1] 指《上都之路》一书。

轮廓中设下一个庞大的海标。如群星般满布诗中的意象无不随着某种形式——某种通过一份艺术规划的演变而成为其形式的形式——的确立而获得了自身的意义与美感。用阿诺德[1]意味深长的话来说，柯勒律治已"让表达服从它旨在表达的东西"。这正是诗歌形式的永恒准则。

然而，有待指出的是，柯勒律治已经白纸黑字，把自己摆在了自己的对立面。1800年，修改后的《古舟子咏》再次出现（在新版《抒情歌谣》里）时，柯勒律治添上了一行副标题："一出诗人幻想（A Poet's Reverie）"。在此，我不抛出任何论点，因为论点显而易见。但这不是一行凭空出现的副标题。忆及1800年版《抒情歌谣》里，还印着《古舟子咏》被华兹华斯一丝不苟地上了编号的四个"重大缺陷"，人们便不难理解柯勒律治的动机。如果连华兹华斯（遑论骚塞）都对《古舟子咏》的艺术熟视无睹，"巴勃尔德夫人们"的无数愚蠢而自满、笃信诗歌必须寓教（教导"'马'是一种动物，'山羊'比'马'更好"）而终，安然等待着机会并时刻准备以"不太可信"来评判诗作的同仁们又该是怎样？无非是把《古舟子咏》视作冒犯，嗤之以"一出幻想"，然后作罢！鉴于柯勒律治受伤的情感，这行被插在正文前的副标题读来像是一份满含恼怒、专为安抚地狱犬的情绪而准备的小礼。虽然到了《女巫之叶》里，柯勒律治就删掉了它，但它已经印出，难以收回，这短短一行小字定期回魂，不断搅扰着柯勒律治的余生。

既不眼盲也不愚蠢的查尔斯·兰姆立刻察觉到"一出诗人幻想"这六个字里的致命含义。在写给华兹华斯的信里，兰姆对华兹华斯的苛刻诗评感到"受伤而气恼"，并就副标题的出现发表了如下看法：

> 我很遗憾，柯勒律治将他的《古舟子咏》命名为"一出诗人幻

---

[1] 马修·阿诺德（Matthew Arnold，1822—1888），英国诗人、批评家。

想"——糟透了,这就像织工波顿[1]在宣称他不是一头狮子,只是一头狮子在舞台上的代表一样。这首诗,它本就由不得我们不信,这行标题除了颠覆它的可信性,颠覆它的真实性,别有何用?

其实,柯勒律治是跳出了煎锅,又栽进了炉火。华兹华斯、骚塞和巴勃尔德夫人会对一部纯属想象的诗作无动于衷,可兰姆和兰姆"部落"却不会。在对付"巴勃尔德那一群人"时,柯勒律治忘了对付他们。

但他同样忘了对付事实。《古舟子咏》是什么都行,但绝不是一出幻想。洛克[2]曾指出:"当'想法'漂浮'心'中,不曾受到'理解'的思考或注意,它就是法国人说的'幻想'(Resvery);我们的'语言'里几乎找不到这样一个词语。"如今,通过简单方便的借用,英语中有了"reverie"。但我们所关心的,不是名称,而是事物本身,洛克对幻想的描述准确无误。在《古舟子咏》成形以前,在它漫长而缓慢的演化过程中,"漂浮"在柯勒律治心中的"想法"时时刻刻都

> 那么稠密,无法尽数,
>   像满居阳光中的绚烂轻尘,
> 也像极了盘桓的梦。[3]

但在《古舟子咏》里,它们不再漂浮:在那摇摆不定、变幻无常的泉涌中,贯穿着一股意识清醒、极具掌控力的能量;它不断接受,不断拒绝,不断塑造、协调着这些想法,让它们和彼此达成一致,和一份清晰的构思达成一致。谈及拉斐尔的《伽拉忒亚》(*Galatea*)

---

1 莎士比亚的戏剧《仲夏夜之梦》里的人物。
2 约翰·洛克(John Locke,1632—1704),英国哲学家。
3 语出英国诗人约翰·弥尔顿(John Milton,1608—1674)的诗作《沉思者》(*Il Penseroso*)。

时，柯勒律治曾提到过"那种营建在'自由生命'的原则和限制性'形式'的原则这两条互相冲突的原则之间的平衡与完美的协调"。在幻想式漂浮意象（其光亮不曾减退分毫）的一瞬自由转化成意象与形式完整性的永恒结合的过程中，隐藏着《古舟子咏》的至美。

约翰·利文斯顿·洛斯

文本说明

  1798年，《古舟子咏》初次发表于首版《抒情歌谣》(*Lyrical Ballads*)。之后，三版《抒情歌谣》（1800、1802、1805年版）重印了修改后的《古舟子咏》。1817年，《古舟子咏》首次署名柯勒律治，由诗选集《女巫之叶》(*Sybilline Leaves*)收录（亦收录于1828年版、1829年版和1834年版）。诗文边注添加于1815年至1816年间（当时，一版柯勒律治诗集正统稿付印），首见于1817年版《女巫之叶》，但这些边注也有可能早已添加完毕。再版于1802年版与1805年版《抒情歌谣》的《古舟子咏》文本与1800年版一致。

我乐于相信，宇宙中不可见的造物多于可见的造物。可谁能为我们解释，这些不可见的存在都属于什么科别？个体的级序如何，关联如何？有什么突出的特征与职能？它们平时都做些什么？又栖居何处？人类的心智始终在探求这方面的知识，却一无所获。当然，我不否认，时而在心中，就像在一块画板上，思量并勾绘一个更大、更好的世界的图景，不令智力因为习于日常生活中的小事而自我窄化并完全没入琐碎的思考，是件颇有裨益的事。但与此同时，我们必须对真理保持警觉，善于把握事物的轻重缓急，以便区分确定与不确定，明辨白昼与黑夜。

——托马斯·伯内特，《考古哲学》，第 68 页

Facile credo, plures esse Naturas invisibiles quam visitbiles in rerum universitate. Sed borum omnium familiam quis nobis-enarrabit? et gradus et cognationes et discrimina et singulorum munera? Quid agunt? quae loca habitant? Harum rerum notitiam semper ambivit ingenium bumanum, nunquam attigit. Juvat, interea, non diffiteor, quandoque in animo, tanquam in tabula, majoris et melioris mundi imaginem contemplari: ne mens assuefacta hodiernae vitae minutiis se contrabat nimis, et tota subsidat in pusillas cogitationes. Sed veritati interea invigilandum est, modusque servandus, ut certa ab incertis, diem a nocte, distinguamus.

T. BURNET, ARCHAEOL. PHIL., P. 68.

古舟子咏
共七个部分

内容提要

  一艘经过赤道的大船如何受暴风雨驱使,闯入雾邦雪国,直抵南极。她如何从南极北行,回到热带纬度,驶入浩瀚的太平洋,经历种种奇异。老水手又以何种方式重返故乡。

How a Ship having passed the Line was driven by storms to the cold Country towards the South Pole; and how from thence she made her course to the tropical Latitude of the Great Pacific Ocean; and of the strange things that befell; and in what manner the Ancyent Marinere came back to his own Country.

第一部分

PART ONE

那是一位年迈的水手,
三人之一被他拦住。
"胡子又白又长,眼睛闪闪发亮,
何以拦我去路?

一位年迈的水手路遇三名应邀参加一场婚宴的翩翩绅士,并拦下了其中一位。

IT is an ancient Mariner,
And he stoppeth one of three.
'By thy long grey beard and glittering eye,
Now wherefore stopp'st thou me?

An ancient Mariner meeteth three Gallants bidden to a wedding-feast, and detaineth one.

新郎的宅院门户大敞。
我是新郎亲属。
宾客都在,大宴将开,
笑闹声就在近处。"

水手伸出枯手,把他抓住,
说"从前有大船一艘"。
"走开!放手,你这白胡子蠢货!"
水手便立刻松开了手。

The Bridegroom's doors are opened wide,
And I am next of kin;
The guests are met, the feast is set:
May'st hear the merry din.'

He holds him with his skinny hand,
'There was a ship,' quoth he.
'Hold off! unhand me, grey-beard loon!'
Eftsoons his hand dropt he.

水手亮起眼睛,把他抓住——
客人两脚发僵,
三岁小孩般竖起了耳朵,
水手如愿以偿。

客人在一块石头上就坐,
他只能乖乖听好。
那年迈的水手目光炯炯,
接着往下说道:

赴宴的客人如着魔一般被远航归来的老水手用眼睛慑住,被迫停下脚步,听他讲述他的故事。

He holds him with his glittering eye—
The Wedding-Guest stood still,
And listens like a three years' child:
The Mariner hath his will.

The Wedding-Guest sat on a stone:
He cannot choose but hear;
And thus spake on that ancient man,
The bright-eyed Mariner.

The Wedding-Guest is spellbound by the eye of the old seafaring man, and constrained to hear his tale.

"人声喧嚷,大船离港,
我们满心舒畅,
驶过教堂,驶过山岗,
驶过塔顶的灯光。

太阳从左边冉冉升起,   水手讲述船儿乘着惠风,在
从大海里升空!   朗朗晴空下航行,一直开到
他光芒耀眼,又从右边   赤道。
沉回大海之中。

'The ship was cheered, the harbour cleared,
Merrily did we drop
Below the kirk, below the hill,
Below the lighthouse top.

The Sun came up upon the left,   The Mariner tells how the
Out of the sea came he!   ship sailed southward with a
And he shone bright, and on the right   good wind and fair weather,
Went down into the sea.   till it reached the line.

他升得一天比一天更高,
午时会挂到桅杆上方——"
客人急得直打胸口,
巴松管乐声嘹亮。

新娘已步入礼堂,   客人听见婚礼的音乐,可水
如玫瑰般红艳;   手仍在讲述。
欢快的乐师点头奏乐,
为她领路在先。

Higher and higher every day,
Till over the mast at noon—'
The Wedding-Guest here beat his breast,
For he heard the loud bassoon.

The bride hath paced into the hall,   The Wedding-Guest heareth
Red as a rose is she;   the bridal music; but the
Nodding their heads before her goes   Mariner continueth his tale.
The merry minstrelsy.

客人急得直打胸口,
却只能乖乖听好。
那年迈的水手目光炯炯,
接着往下说道:

"然后,暴风雨袭来,
来得凶猛而猖狂: 船被一股风暴赶向南极。
他甩开翅膀,横冲直撞,
把我们赶向南方。

The Wedding-Guest he beat his breast,
Yet he cannot choose but hear;
And thus spake on that ancient man,
The bright-eyed Mariner.

'And now the STORM-BLAST came, and he
Was tyrannous and strong:
He struck with his o'ertaking wings, The ship driven by a storm
And chased us south along. toward the south pole.

就那么弓着船桅，低着船首，
好像吆喝与棍棒紧追在后，
步步踩在敌影里头，
脖子向前一弯，
船儿埋头飞窜，风雨咆哮不断，
我们一路向南逃难。

直到大雾弥漫，雪花飘落，
伴着刺骨奇寒。
寒冰举起高樯，从旁漂过，
绿如翡翠一般。

With sloping masts and dipping prow,
As who pursued with yell and blow
Still treads the shadow of his foe,
And forward bends his head,
The ship drove fast, loud roared the blast,
And southward aye we fled.

And now there came both mist and snow,
And it grew wondrous cold:
And ice, mast-high, came floating by,
As green as emerald.

浮冰之间，那雪白的冰山

透出瘆人的光彩：

没一个人影、一声兽鸣——

冰块连着冰块。

这儿是冰，那儿是冰，

冰无处不在。

时而爆裂，低嚎，呼吼，咆哮，

这迷中万籁[1]！

终于在冰海上空，一只信天翁

穿越迷雾而来。

> 冰雪之国，没有活物的踪迹，只有冰块、冰山和可怖的声响。

And through the drifts the snowy clifts

Did send a dismal sheen:

Nor shapes of men nor beasts we ken—

The ice was all between.

The ice was here, the ice was there,

The ice was all around:

It cracked and growled, and roared and howled,

Like noises in a swound!

At length did cross an Albatross,

Thorough the fog it came;

> The land of ice, and of fearful sounds where no living thing was to be seen.

---

[1] "迷中万籁"指在晕厥过程中听到的种种声响，此处为控制诗歌节奏，译为"迷中万籁"。

我们像见了耶稣的门徒，
由衷向它喝彩。

它吃掉它从没吃过的食物，
一圈、一圈地飞。
一阵雷鸣传来，冰牢裂开，
舵手率船突围！

爽快的南风在身后吹起，
信天翁日夜相随，
水手们一叫，它就来报到，
为了玩伴和美味！

终于，一只名为信天翁的巨大海鸟穿越雪雾而来，船员们不胜欣喜，热情地接待了它。

瞧！这信天翁无疑是吉祥的征兆，它紧跟大船，一路北归，穿越浓雾与浮冰。

As if it had been a Christian soul,
We hailed it in God's name.

It ate the food it ne'er had eat,
And round and round it flew.
The ice did split with a thunder-fit;
The helmsman steered us through!

And a good south wind sprung up behind;
The Albatross did follow,
And every day, for food or play,
Came to the mariners' hollo!

Till a great sea-bird, called the Albatross, came through the snow-fog, and was received with great joy and hospitality.

And lo! the Albatross proveth a bird of good omen, and followeth the ship as it returned northward through fog and floating ice.

连着九晚,云遮雾染,

它在桅杆桅索上栖宿。

整整九夜,那微白的冷月

都披着层层白雾。"

"上帝保佑,老水手哟!

别让魔鬼再把你折磨!——

怎么这副面容?"——"我用十字弓

射死了信天翁。"

> 老水手无情地杀死了善良而真诚的吉鸟。

In mist or cloud, on mast or shroud,

It perched for vespers nine;

Whiles all the night, through fog-smoke white,

Glimmered the white Moon-shine.'

'God save thee, ancient Mariner!

From the fiends, that plague thee thus!—

Why look'st thou so?' — 'With my cross-bow

I shot the ALBATROSS. '

> The ancient Mariner inhospitably killeth the pious bird of good omen.

太阳开始从右边升起:
从大海里升空

第二部分

PART TWO

太阳开始从右边升起:
从大海里升空,
依稀掩在雾里,从左边
沉回大海之中。

    THE Sun now rose upon the right:
    Out of the sea came he,
    Still hid in mist, and on the left
    Went down into the sea.

爽快的南风吹在身后，
却没了那可爱的大鸟，
水手们放声喊开，它也不再
把玩伴和美味寻找！

我犯下不可饶恕的罪过，   同船的人大声斥责老水
怕要连累全船的弟兄。   手，怪他杀死了带来好运
他们都说，我闯了大祸，   的大鸟。
是这大鸟带来了南风。
你倒好，混蛋！你杀了神鸟，
是它带来了南风！

And the good south wind still blew behind,
But no sweet bird did follow,
Nor any day for food or play
Came to the mariners' hollo!

And I had done a hellish thing,   His shipmates cry out against
And it would work 'em woe: the ancient Mariner, for
For all averred, I had killed the bird   killing the bird of good luck.
That made the breeze to blow.
Ah wretch! said they, the bird to slay,
That made the breeze to blow!

不暗不红,如上帝金首,
太阳破雾而出。
他们又说,你没做错,
是这大鸟掀起了大雾。
你做得很好,杀了这鬼鸟,
是它掀起了大雾。

可当迷雾散去,他们又改口为老水手辩护,从而让自己成为帮凶。

和风吹拂,白沫飞舞,
船儿踏波逐浪。
我们闯入那片无人涉足、
没有声息的海洋。

和风继续吹送;大船进入太平洋海域,仍不断北行,抵达赤道后亦无转向。

Nor dim nor red, like God's own head,
The glorious Sun uprist:
Then all averred, I had killed the bird
That brought the fog and mist.
'Twas right, said they, such birds to slay,
That bring the fog and mist.

But when the fog cleared off, they justify the same, and thus make themselves accomplices in the crime.

The fair breeze blew, the white foam flew,
The furrow followed free;
We were the first that ever burst
Into that silent sea.

The fair breeze continues; the ship enters the Pacific Ocean, and sails northward, even till it reaches the Line.

南风止歇,瘪了风帆,   突然,风止船停。
一片冷冷戚戚。
我们找起话说,只想打破
这茫茫沉寂!

正午时分,正对桅顶,
那血红的太阳高高
悬在铜黄、炙热的天空,
月亮般大小。

Down dropt the breeze, the sails dropt down,   The ship hath been suddenly becalmed.
'Twas sad as sad could be;
And we did speak only to break
The silence of the sea!

All in a hot and copper sky,
The bloody Sun, at noon,
Right up above the mast did stand,
No bigger than the Moon.

一天一天，一天一天，
船纹丝不动，
静得像艘画里的船，
停在画里的海中。

水呀，水呀，到处是水， 　　　　　　　　　　　杀鸟之后，报应开始。
船板片片起皱；
水呀，水呀，到处是水，
一滴也喝不下口。

Day after day, day after day,
We stuck, nor breath nor motion;
As idle as a painted ship
Upon a painted ocean.

Water, water, every where,　　　　　　　　　And the Albatross begins to
And all the boards did shrink;　　　　　　　be avenged.
Water, water, every where,
Nor any drop to drink.

船下是万丈腐海。耶稣啊!
怎有如此海天!
嘀,那黏滑的活物爬进爬出,
爬满了黏滑的海面。

鬼火冥光,成圈成行,
夜夜飞旋起舞。
海水绿了又蓝,蓝了又白,
像女巫的滚滚沸油。

The very deep did rot: O Christ!
That ever this should be!
Yea, slimy things did crawl with legs
Upon the slimy sea.

About, about, in reel and rout
The death-fires danced at night;
The water, like a witch's oils,
Burnt green, and blue and white.

有人在梦中确信，有灵怪
在把我们陷害。
它从雪雾之乡远远跟来，
藏在九寻深海。

没一滴水露，渴得舌头
都连根枯萎。
我们发不出声响，好像
喉咙噎着煤灰。

一个幽灵从南极跟来，它是这个星球上的隐形居民之一，既非亡者的灵魂，亦非神国的天使。关于这些隐形的居民，可以参考博学的犹太人约瑟夫斯和君士坦丁堡的柏拉图主义者米哈伊尔·塞洛斯的说法与著作。它们为数众多，难以细数，任何环境里都有它们的存在。

And some in dreams assurèd were
Of the Spirit that plagued us so;
Nine fathom deep he had followed us
From the land of mist and snow.

And every tongue, through utter drought,
Was withered at the root;
We could not speak, no more than if
We had been choked with soot.

A Spirit had followed them; one of the invisible inhabitants of this planet, neither departed souls nor angels; concerning whom the learned Jew, Josephus, and the Platonic Constantinopolitan, Michael Psellus, may be consulted. They are very numerous, and there is no climate or element, without one or more.

哎！要命！全船老小
目光何等哀怨！
他们把死鸟当作十字，
挂在我的颈间。

船上众人痛苦难挨，自然很愿意把所有罪责都推到老水手身上：他们把大鸟的尸体挂上他的脖子，以示咎责。

Ah! well a-day! what evil looks
Had I from old and young!
Instead of the cross, the Albatross
About my neck was hung.

The shipmates, in their sore distress, would fain throw the whole guilt on the ancient Mariner: in sign whereof they hang the dead sea-bird round his neck.

赤裸的船架靠到近旁,
他们又把骰子一抛

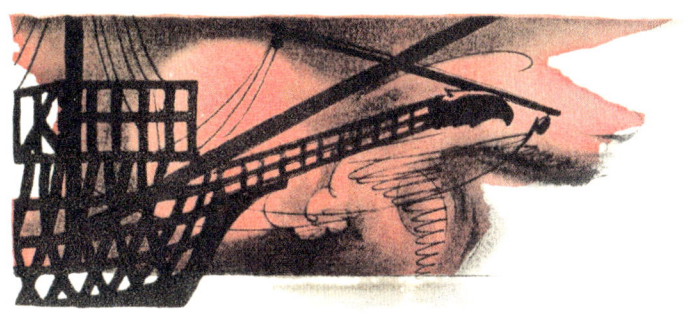

第三部分

PART THREE

那阵子实在太苦。一副副
冒火的喉咙、呆子的眼珠。
实在太苦!实在太苦!
呆苦呆苦的眼珠,
好歹往西边一转,我望见
天上不知何物。

遥望远天,老水手看见异物的迹象。

THERE passed a weary time. Each throat
Was parched, and glazed each eye.
A weary time! a weary time!
How glazed each weary eye,
When looking westward, I beheld
A something in the sky.

The ancient Mariner beholdeth a sign in the element afar off.

起初它像个小小的斑点，
接着像一团水汽。
它东游西晃，动了又动，
最终显出了形体。

斑点、水汽和那最后的形体！
它离得越来越近。
它上蹿下跳，左弯右拐，
像在闪躲水里的妖精。

At first it seemed a little speck,
And then it seemed a mist;
It moved and moved, and took at last
A certain shape, I wist.

A speck, a mist, a shape, I wist!
And still it neared and neared:
As if it dodged a water-sprite,
It plunged and tacked and veered.

嘴唇焦黑,喉咙堵着煤灰,
我们哭笑两难,
渴得个个像哑巴似的站着!
我咬破胳膊,吸了口血,
才喊出,有船!有船!

异物越来越近,在老水手看来,它似乎是一条大船。他付出重大的代价,挣脱干渴的禁锢,终于喊出声来。

嘴唇焦黑,喉咙堵着煤灰,
他们目瞪口呆:
一听有船,谢天谢地!
个个笑开了嘴,大口地吸气,
像要喝个畅快。

一闪喜悦。

With throats unslaked, with black lips baked,
We could nor laugh nor wail;
Through utter drought all dumb we stood!
I bit my arm, I sucked the blood,
And cried, A sail! a sail!

At its nearer approach, it seemeth him to be a ship; and at a dear ransom he freeth his speech from the bonds of thirst.

With throats unslaked, with black lips baked,
Agape they heard me call:
Gramercy! they for joy did grin,
And all at once their breath drew in.
As they were drinking all.

A flash of joy;

（我喊着）看啊！看啊！她不再拐弯！

她是救我们来的。

没一丝海风、一层海浪，

她竟直挺挺地来了！

西边的海波像熊熊焰火。

又要迎来夜晚！

太阳倚着西边的海波，

又大又亮又圆。

那船形的怪物突然出现，

开到我们和太阳之间。

恐怖紧随其后。没风没浪，船又何以疾航？

See! see! (I cried) she tacks no more!

Hither to work us weal;

Without a breeze, without a tide,

She steadies with upright keel!

The western wave was all a-flame.

The day was well nigh done!

Almost upon the western wave

Rested the broad bright Sun;

When that strange shape drove suddenly

Betwixt us and the Sun.

And horror follows. For can it be a ship that comes onward without wind or tide?

太阳蒙上道道黑影,   在他看来,那就是一条船
(天堂圣母垂怜!)   的骨架。
他仿佛从地牢的栅栏后面
露出了火热的大脸。

天啊!(我想,心怦怦直跳)
她越来越近,快得可怕!
像摇晃的蛛网一样闪着光的
就是*她*的帆吗?

And straight the Sun was flecked with bars,   It seemeth him but the skeleton
(Heaven's Mother send us grace!)   of a ship.
As if through a dungeon-grate he peered
With broad and burning face.

Alas! (thought I, and my heart beat loud)
How fast she nears and nears!
Are those *her* sails that glance in the Sun,
Like restless gossameres?

像牢栏一样挡着太阳的

就是她的肋骨？

船上就那一个女子？

还是两个？另一个莫非是"死"？

"死"是那女子的大副？

它的肋骨像根根栏杆一样贴在夕阳脸上。

骨架上只有那幽鬼般的女子和她的"死"伴，别无一物。

一女一"死"，好像船长大副！

她唇色红艳，神情放纵，

金发熠熠满头。

她肤色惨白，如害麻风，

她是名叫"死中之生"的噩梦，

能以冰寒冻人血流。

Are those *her* ribs through which the Sun

Did peer, as through a grate?

And is that Woman all her crew?

Is that a DEATH? and are there two?

Is DEATH that woman's mate?

And its ribs are seen as bars on the face of the setting Sun.

The Spectre-Woman and her Death-mate, and no other on board the skeleton ship.

Like vessel, like crew!

Her lips were red, *her* looks were free,

Her locks were yellow as gold:

Her skin was as white as leprosy,

The Night-mare LIFE-IN-DEATH was she,

Who thicks man's blood with cold.

赤裸的船架靠到近旁,
他们又把骰子一抛。
"这局结束!我赢了!我赢了!"
说着她吹了三声口哨。

"死"与"死中之生"掷骰赌博,以全体船员为彩头,她(后者)赢得了老水手。

红日落海,群星奔涌:
暗夜霎时降临。
鬼船疾疾驶去,海上
传来遥遥低吟。

海天之间,暮光已尽。

The naked hulk alongside came,
And the twain were casting dice;
'The game is done! I've won! I've won!'
Quoth she, and whistles thrice.

Death and Life-in-Death have diced for the ship's crew, and she (the latter) winneth the ancient Mariner.

The Sun's rim dips; the stars rush out:
At one stride comes the dark;
With far-heard whisper, o'er the sea,
Off shot the spectre-bark.

No twilight within the courts of the Sun.

我们边听边斜目远眺!

恐惧在我心头,似要

把心血饮啜!

群星暗淡,夜色深浓,

灯下是舵手煞白的面孔。

露水从帆上滴落——

直到新月爬上东方的天际,   月亮升起,

一颗明星被月尖钩起,

在月弯里闪烁。

We listened and looked sideways up!

Fear at my heart, as at a cup,

My life-blood seemed to sip!

The stars were dim, and thick the night,

The steersman's face by his lamp gleamed white;

From the sails the dew did drip—

Till clomb above the eastern bar   At the rising of the Moon,

The hornèd Moon, with one bright star

Within the nether tip.

来不及呻吟叹息，便有剧痛
随着月移星走，
把人接连击中，人人转脸　　　　　　　一个接着一个，
用眼睛把我诅咒。

五十有四，两百个活人，
（全无呻吟叹息）
伴着嘭嘭直响，像木头一样　　　　　同船的水手倒地而亡。
一个一个倒地。

One after one, by the star-dogged Moon,
Too quick for groan or sigh,
Each turned his face with a ghastly pang,　　One after another,
And cursed me with his eye.

Four times fifty living men,
(And I heard nor sigh nor groan)
With heavy thump, a lifeless lump,　　His shipmates drop down dead.
They dropped down one by one.

灵魂从他们的身体里飞走，——
飞向幸福或灾祸！
每一个灵魂都像弩箭嗖嗖，   "死中之生"开始把老水手
从我身边掠过！   耍弄。

The souls did from their bodies fly,—
They fled to bliss or woe!
And every soul, it passed me by,
Like the whizz of my cross-bow!   But Life-in-Death begins her work on the ancient Mariner.

只有，只有，只有我一人
面对淼淼海波

第四部分

PART FOUR

"我怕你,年迈的水手!   赴宴的客人胆战心惊,怕
我害怕你枯瘦的手!   是一个幽灵在跟他说话。
你又细又长,浑身蜡黄,
好像海沙起了棱皱。

'I FEAR thee, ancient Mariner!   The Wedding-Guest feareth that a
I fear thy skinny hand!   Spirit is talking to him;
And thou art long, and lank, and brown,
As is the ribbed sea-sand.

我怕你，怕你闪亮的眼睛
和你焦黄、枯瘦的手。"——
别怕，别怕，婚宴的宾客！
我还没栽跟头。

只有，只有，只有我一人
面对淼淼海波！
没一位仙神，来可怜
我痛苦的魂魄。

但老水手让客人相信他是
血肉之躯，又继续讲起他
遭受的可怕惩罚。

I fear thee and thy glittering eye,
And thy skinny hand, so brown.' —
Fear not, fear not, thou Wedding-Guest!
This body dropt not down.

Alone, alone, all, all alone,
Alone on a wide wide sea!
And never a saint took pity on
My soul in agony.

But the ancient Mariner assureth him of his bodily life, and proceedeth to relate his horrible penance.

那么多人,如此俊美!

无不横尸船上。

千千万万黏滑的生物　　　　　　　他厌恶海里的生物,

存活如故;我也一样。

我望一眼腐烂的大海,　　　　　　继而生出嫉妒,心想这么

转头把视线挪走;　　　　　　　　多人横尸船上,这些东西

我望一眼腐烂的甲板,　　　　　　竟还活着。

一地死去的水手。

The many men, so beautiful!

And they all dead did lie:

And a thousand thousand slimy things　　He despiseth the creatures of the

Lived on; and so did I.　　　　　　　　 calm,

I looked upon the rotting sea,　　　　 And envieth that they should live,

And drew my eyes away;　　　　　　　 and so many lie dead.

I looked upon the rotting deck,

And there the dead men lay.

我仰望上天，试着祷告；
谁料只字未进，
便传来一声恶毒的低咒，
让我心灰意冷。

我闭上眼睛，不敢睁开，
眼珠像脉搏似的蹦跳；
因为沉沉天海，沉沉海天，
会压向我疲惫的双眼，
还有死尸困我双脚。

I looked to Heaven, and tried to pray;
But or ever a prayer had gusht,
A wicked whisper came, and made
My heart as dry as dust.

I closed my lids, and kept them close,
And the balls like pulses beat;
For the sky and the sea, and the sea and the sky
Lay like a load on my weary eye,
And the dead were at my feet.

冷汗从死人的四肢上消融，

他们不烂、不臭，

看我的眼神哀怨依旧，

不曾被死亡带走。

孤儿的诅咒，能把灵魂

从天国拽进地府。

可喔！比那更可怕的，

是死人眼里的诅咒！

七天七宿，我受尽折磨，

却一死难求。

> 对老水手的诅咒依然活在死者眼中。

The cold sweat melted from their limbs,
Nor rot nor reek did they:
The look with which they looked on me
Had never passed away.

An orphan's curse would drag to hell
A spirit from on high;
But oh! more horrible than that
Is the curse in a dead man's eye!
Seven days, seven nights, I saw that curse,
And yet I could not die.

> But the curse liveth for him in the eye of the dead men.

月亮移步，登上高空，
一处也不肯停留。
她悄悄升起，有一两颗星
时时伴她左右——

月光如四月银霜般洒下，
嘲笑着闷热的海。
船身投下巨大的影子，
着魔的海水燃烧不止，
红得沉静、可骇。

孤单一人，浑身僵硬，他汲汲望向高空，望着夜月，望着看似静停，实则随月而动的星辰。深蓝的夜空每一寸都属于星月，它是为星月而设的床榻，是它们的母国和与生俱来的家园，而身为主人，它们无需声明，便能理所当然、满受期待地走进家门，带着一种静静的喜悦。

The moving Moon went up the sky,
And no where did abide:
Softly she was going up,
And a star or two beside—

Her beams bemocked the sultry main,
Like April hoar-frost spread;
But where the ship's huge shadow lay,
The charmèd water burnt alway
A still and awful red.

In his loneliness and fixedness he yearneth towards the journeying Moon, and the stars that still sojourn, yet still move onward; and every where the blue sky belongs to them, and is their appointed rest, and their native country and their own natural homes, which they enter unannounced, as lords that are certainly expected and yet there is a silent joy at their arrival.

在船影之外,我望见

条条水蛇游曳:

水中亮起皎白的踪迹,

那幽幽灵光,当它们竖起身体,

像莹莹飘雪。

在船影里面,我看见

蛇群色彩斑斓:

青蓝、油绿,柔绒般黑滑,

每条都尽情舒卷,留下

金色的火光一闪。

借着月光,他看见上帝的造物在大海里徜徉。

Beyond the shadow of the ship,
I watched the water-snakes:
They moved in tracks of shining white,
And when they reared, the elfish light
Fell off in hoary flakes.

Within the shadow of the ship
I watched their rich attire:
Blue, glossy green, and velvet black,
They coiled and swam; and every track
Was a flash of golden fire.

By the light of the Moon he beholdeth God's creatures of the great calm.

多么快乐的生灵！美得 　　　　　　　海蛇的美与欢乐。
没有言语能描述。
爱的甘泉从心底涌起，
不觉间，我送上了祝福，
准是慈悲的天神垂怜于我，　　　他在心里为它们祝福。
不觉间，我送上了祝福。

那一刻，我终于能开口祷告；　　魔咒开始破除。
脖子又能自由转动，
信天翁掉落，像铅一样
直直坠入海中。

     O happy living things! no tongue   Their beauty and their happiness.
     Their beauty might declare:
     A spring of love gushed from my heart,
     And I blessed them unaware:
     Sure my kind saint took pity on me,   He blesseth them in his heart.
     And I blessed them unaware.

     The self-same moment I could pray;   The spell begins to break.
     And from my neck so free
     The Albatross fell off, and sank
     Like lead into the sea.

一哼，一动，一个个站起，
却没人说话、转眼

第五部分

PART FIVE

喔,酣眠!天下无人
不爱你的温存!
为天堂圣母献上礼赞!
她把你的温存送到人间,
让你溜进我的心魂。

OH sleep! it is a gentle thing,
Beloved from pole to pole!
To Mary Queen the praise be given!
She sent the gentle sleep from Heaven,
That slid into my soul.

甲板上，只只呆蠢的水桶
空了不知几天。
我梦见它们接满了水露，
醒来时，天降雨点。

我嘴唇潮润，喉咙冰凉，
衣服都已湿透，
准是梦里就喝了很多，
醒来还喝个不休。

圣母垂怜，天降甘霖，老水手一解焦渴。

The silly buckets on the deck,
That had so long remained,
I dreamt that they were filled with dew;
And when I awoke, it rained.

My lips were wet, my throat was cold,
My garments all were dank;
Sure I had drunken in my dreams,
And still my body drank.

By grace of the holy Mother, the ancient Mariner is refreshed with rain.

一动，却感觉不到手脚。
我浑身轻飘——真真
像已在美妙的梦中死掉，
成了幸福的游魂。

很快，我听见风的咆哮。　　　他听见风声，看见海上、
它不曾吹到近旁，　　　　　　空中出现了奇怪的景象与
但那张张脆薄的枯帆　　　　　骚动。
已在风声里摇晃。

I moved, and could not feel my limbs:
I was so light—almost
I thought that I had died in sleep,
And was a blessèd ghost.

And soon I heard a roaring wind:　　He heareth sounds and seeth
It did not come anear;　　　　　　　strange sights and commotions in
But with its sound it shook the sails,　the sky and the element.
That were so thin and sere.

天空忽然生机勃发！
百来面火旗闪闪，
来来去去，形色匆匆，
惨白的星在火光中舞动，
来来去去，忽明忽暗。

风的咆哮越发狂暴，
船帆如萧萧莎草。
一块乌云把雨水倾倒，
和月亮紧紧相靠。

The upper air burst into life!
And a hundred fire-flags sheen,
To and fro they were hurried about!
And to and fro, and in and out,
The wan stars danced between.

And the coming wind did roar more loud,
And the sails did sigh like sedge;
And the rain poured down from one black cloud;
The Moon was at its edge.

那厚厚的乌云裂成两半,

月亮仍在云畔。

闪电不打一弯,似瀑布般

径直冲下高高的崖岩,

拉开陡阔的银川。

狂风从未触碰船帆,   船员的尸体被唤醒,船

船却开始前行!   始移动。

月川之下,死去的水手

发出一阵哼鸣。

The thick black cloud was cleft, and still

The Moon was at its side:

Like waters shot from some high crag,

The lightning fell with never a jag,

A river steep and wide.

The loud wind never reached the ship,   The bodies of the ship's crew are

Yet now the ship moved on!   inspired and the ship moves on;

Beneath the lightning and the Moon

The dead men gave a groan.

一哼,一动,一个个站起,
却没人说话、转眼。
人死了又起,换在梦里,
也是怪事一件。

舵手掌舵,船儿奔游。
没一丝海风,
水手们开始工作,照旧
忙着把绳索拉送。
他们举起木头般的胳膊——
一船幽魂返工。

They groaned, they stirred, they all uprose,
Nor spake, nor moved their eyes;
It had been strange, even in a dream,
To have seen those dead men rise.

The helmsman steered, the ship moved on;
Yet never a breeze up-blew;
The mariners all 'gan work the ropes,
Where they were wont to do;
They raised their limbs like lifeless tools—
We were a ghastly crew.

我侄儿的身体紧挨着我,
膝头对着膝头。
他和我同拉一条绳索,
可始终没向我开口。

"我怕你,年迈的水手!"
镇定,客人,镇定!
不是那苦苦逃遁的游魂
此刻又重回尸身,那是一群
被祝福的精灵。

但唤醒尸体的,并非船员的灵魂,也非大地精灵与空中精灵,而是应守护圣徒的祈祷从天而降的一群天使之灵。

The body of my brother's son
Stood by me, knee to knee:
The body and I pulled at one rope,
But he said nought to me.

'I fear thee, ancient Mariner!'
Be calm, thou Wedding-Guest!
'Twas not those souls that fled in pain,
Which to their corses came again,
But a troop of spirits blest:

But not by the souls of the men, nor by demons of earth or middle air, but by a blessed troop of angelic spirits, sent down by the invocation of the guardian saint.

天亮时——他们放下胳膊,

一齐向桅杆聚拢。

徐徐清歌从他们的唇间涌出,

向四面八方飘动。

一众美妙的歌声圈圈飞升,

猛地冲向太阳;

接着,又缓缓落回海上,

时而独唱,时而和响。

For when it dawned — they dropped their arms,

And clustered round the mast;

Sweet sounds rose slowly through their mouths,

And from their bodies passed.

Around, around, flew each sweet sound,

Then darted to the Sun;

Slowly the sounds came back again,

Now mixed, now one by one.

有时我听见云雀的鸣啭

兀然从天而降。

有时是无数小鸟的啁啾,

长空大海之间,简直

满是甜美的欢唱!

有时,如有琴瑟万千,

有时是孤笛一把。

最后,一曲天使之歌

令九天俱哑。

Sometimes a-dropping from the sky

I heard the sky-lark sing;

Sometimes all little birds that are,

How they seemed to fill the sea and air

With their sweet jargoning!

And now 'twas like all instruments,

Now like a lonely flute;

And now it is an angel's song,

That makes the heavens be mute.

歌声止歇。可直到中午，
帆声依然悦耳，
仿佛在绿意葱茏的六月，
躲进浓荫的小河，
整夜整夜，向沉睡的森林
唱着安静的歌。

直到中午，我们安然前行，
海上无一缕风息：
船开得缓慢、平静，
借着水下的助力。

It ceased; yet still the sails made on
A pleasant noise till noon,
A noise like of a hidden brook
In the leafy month of June,
That to the sleeping woods all night
Singeth a quiet tune.

Till noon we quietly sailed on,
Yet never a breeze did breathe:
Slowly and smoothly went the ship,
Moved onward from beneath.

船身之下,九寻深海,
那灵怪仍在。是他
从雪雾之乡悄悄跟来,
推着我们向前进发。
到了正午,船帆罢了吟唱,
船也彻底停下。

太阳高挂,正对桅顶,
船被牢牢定住:
可没过多久,她又开始移动,
动得忐忑而短促——
一前一后,每次半个身长,
动得忐忑而短促。

> 孤独的水下精灵服从天使们的命令,将大船从南极推至赤道,但他仍想复仇。

Under the keel nine fathom deep,
From the land of mist and snow,
The spirit slid: and it was he
That made the ship to go.
The sails at noon left off their tune,
And the ship stood still also.

The Sun, right up above the mast,
Had fixed her to the ocean:
But in a minute she 'gan stir,
With a short uneasy motion—
Backwards and forwards half her length
With a short uneasy motion.

> The lonesome Spirit from the south-pole carries on the ship as far as the Line, in obedience to the angelic troop, but still requireth vengeance.

接着,她突然挺身一跃,
像匹脱缰的烈马。
全身的血液灌进脑海,
我在迷眩中倒下。

躺在那儿,昏迷了多久,
我也说不分明;
不过,在知觉恢复之前,
我便听见,心中也能分辨,
空中有两个声音。

Then like a pawing horse let go,
She made a sudden bound:
It flung the blood into my head,
And I fell down in a swound.

How long in that same fit I lay,
I have not to declare;
But ere my living life returned,
I heard and in my soul discerned
Two voices in the air.

一个说:"是这人吗?告诉我,
凭着耶稣的名义,是他
用无情的弓弩,一箭射死了
善良的信天翁吗?

那独居雪雾之乡的灵怪
对这鸟儿喜爱至深,
而这鸟儿却偏偏爱上
这取他性命的恶人。"

极地精灵的同类,海天之间的隐形居民,也参与进来,评判罪罚。其中两位的声音传来,一位对另一位讲起,针对老水手的漫长而沉重的惩罚已被授予极地精灵,极地精灵已向南回转。

'Is it he?' quoth one, 'Is this the man?
By him who died on cross,
With his cruel bow he laid full low
The harmless Albatross.

The spirit who bideth by himself
In the land of mist and snow,
He loved the bird that loved the man
Who shot him with his bow.'

The Polar Spirit's fellow-demons, the invisible inhabitants of the element, take part in his wrong; and two of them relate, one to the other, that penance long and heavy for the ancient Mariner hath been accorded to the Polar Spirit, who returneth southward.

另一个声音更加温柔,

似汩汩蜜露:

他说:"此人已受到惩罚,

惩罚还没有结束。"

The other was a softer voice,

As soft as honey-dew:

Quoth he, 'The man hath penance done,

And penance more will do.'

我无法躲开他们的目光,
也无法抬头祈祷

第六部分

PART SIX

第一个声音

"说呀,说呀!再让我听听
你那温柔的声音——
船开得飞快,是什么原因?
大海可曾使劲?"

First Voice

'BUT tell me, tell me! speak again,
Thy soft response renewing—
What makes that ship drive on so fast?
What is the ocean doing?'

第二个声音

"大海像仆人一般温顺,
不起半点风浪。
他默默亮着巨大的眼睛,
看着天上的月亮——

何去何从,祸福吉凶;
全听月亮指示。
看呀!兄台,看她俯望大海,
目光多么仁慈。"

Second Voice

'Still as a slave before his lord,
The ocean hath no blast;
His great bright eye most silently
Up to the Moon is cast—

If he may know which way to go;
For she guides him smooth or grim.
See, brother, see! how graciously
She looketh down on him.'

第一个声音

"可既没海风,又没海浪,
船怎么快成这样?"

老水手被掷入恍惚。天使的力量让大船以人类无法承受的速度向北航行。

第二个声音

"船头的空气从中切开,
到船尾合成一块。

飞呀!老兄,飞上高高的天空!
时间已经不起耽误。
一会儿那水手梦醒之后,
船就会慢慢减速。"

First Voice

'But why drives on that ship so fast,
Without or wave or wind?'

The Mariner hath been cast into a trance; for the angelic power causeth the vessel to drive northward faster than human life could endure.

Second Voice

'The air is cut away before,
And closes from behind.

Fly, brother, fly! more high, more high!
Or we shall be belated:
For slow and slow that ship will go,
When the Mariner's trance is abated.'

我清醒过来,船继续前行,
一如风轻浪细的时候。
那宁静的夜晚,夜月高悬,
死者在月下聚首。

所有人都站在一起,甲板上
倒像个地下灵堂。
所有人都紧盯着我,冰冷的眼眸
闪出道道寒光。

超自然力量退去。老水手醒来,惩罚重新开始。

I woke, and we were sailing on
As in a gentle weather:
'Twas night, calm night, the moon was high;
The dead men stood together.

All stood together on the deck,
For a charnel-dungeon fitter:
All fixed on me their stony eyes,
That in the Moon did glitter.

The supernatural motion is retarded; the Mariner awakes, and his penance begins anew.

他们临死时的剧痛与诅咒，
从未消减分毫：
我无法躲开他们的目光，
也无法抬头祈祷。

魔咒戛然消止。我再次　　　　　　　　　　诅咒终被解开。
望向碧蓝的海洋，
又举目远眺，却再难见到
那些熟悉的景象——

The pang, the curse, with which they died,
Had never passed away:
I could not draw my eyes from theirs,
Nor turn them up to pray.

And now this spell was snapt: once more　　The curse is finally expiated.
I viewed the ocean green,
And looked far forth, yet little saw
Of what had else been seen—

就像有人胆怯心慌,

在无人的僻路上行走,

转身看上一眼,便只顾向前,

再也不敢回头。

因为他知道,有个可怕的恶魔

紧紧跟在身后。

但很快,一阵清风吹来,

没半点响动。

它未曾打海面上经过,

没一丝影踪。

      Like one, that on a lonesome road

      Doth walk in fear and dread,

      And having once turned round walks on,

      And turns no more his head;

      Because he knows, a frightful fiend

      Doth close behind him tread.

      But soon there breathed a wind on me,

      Nor sound nor motion made:

      Its path was not upon the sea,

      In ripple or in shade.

它撩起头发,拂过脸颊,
像春风吹过草场——
怪哉!它和我心中的恐惧交融,
又对我张开臂膀。

船开得飞快、飞快,
却无一阵颠簸;
风吹得轻柔、轻柔,
却只把我抚摸。

It raised my hair, it fanned my cheek
Like a meadow-gale of spring—
It mingled strangely with my fears,
Yet it felt like a welcoming.

Swiftly, swiftly flew the ship,
Yet she sailed softly too:
Sweetly, sweetly blew the breeze—
On me alone it blew.

喔！这甜美的幻梦！这真是

那塔顶的灯光？

是那山岗？是那教堂？

这真是我的故乡？

漂过浅滩，船儿进湾，

我哭着向天祈愿——

上帝啊！叫醒我吧！不然，

请让我就此长眠。

老水手看见故乡。

Oh! dream of joy! is this indeed

The light-house top I see?

Is this the hill? is this the kirk?

Is this mine own countree?

We drifted o'er the harbour-bar,

And I with sobs did pray—

O let me be awake, my God!

Or let me sleep alway.

And the ancient Mariner beholdeth his native country.

故乡的港湾明净如镜,
铺得如此顺滑!
皎洁的月光挽起月影,
向平静的海面倾洒。

山岩闪闪发光,山上
是同样闪亮的教堂。
风标纹丝不动,昂首
沐浴着静静的月光。

The harbour-bay was clear as glass,
So smoothly it was strewn!
And on the bay the moonlight lay,
And the shadow of the Moon.

The rock shone bright, the kirk no less,
That stands above the rock:
The moonlight steeped in silentness
The steady weathercock.

海面染上岑岑白亮,
谁料须臾之间,
一众形影闪着红光　　　　　　　天使之灵离开尸体,
纷纷从水中涌现。

成群的红影就在那里,　　　　　　闪着红光,显出原本的
在离船头不远的地方。　　　　　　形体。
我回头望向甲板——天啊!
那是什么景象!

And the bay was white with silent light,
Till rising from the same,
Full many shapes, that shadows were,   The angelic spirits leave the
In crimson colours came.   dead bodies,

A little distance from the prow   And appear in their own
Those crimson shadows were: forms of light.
I turned my eyes upon the deck—
Oh, Christ! what saw I there!

地上躺满尸体，了无生气，
可凭着圣十字起誓！
每具尸体上面，都站着一个
红光遍体的天使。

一班天使，个个把手挥起，
好一派天国景貌！
他们像盏盏可爱的红灯，
向陆地发出信号。

Each corse lay flat, lifeless and flat,
And, by the holy rood!
A man all light, a seraph-man,
On every corse there stood.

This seraph-band, each waved his hand:
It was a heavenly sight!
They stood as signals to the land,
Each one a lovely light;

一班天使,个个把手挥起,
没出任何声音——
一声不响。可喔!那寂静
像音乐一样沁入我心。

可很快,我听见桨声欸乃,
听见领港人的呼喊。
我不由自主地转过脑袋,
看见一条小船。

This seraph-band, each waved his hand,
No voice did they impart—
No voice; but oh! the silence sank
Like music on my heart.

But soon I heard the dash of oars,
I heard the Pilot's cheer;
My head was turned perforce away
And I saw a boat appear.

来的是领港人和他的小孩,

我听见他们来得飞快。

伟大的上帝！我心中的欣喜

再多尸体也没法破坏。

船上还有一人——听声音，

是那隐士大德！

他朗朗放声，虔诚地唱起

在林中谱写的圣歌。

他将洗净信天翁的血迹，

赦免我灵魂的罪恶。

The Pilot and the Pilot's boy,

I heard them coming fast:

Dear Lord in Heaven! it was a joy

The dead men could not blast.

I saw a third—I heard his voice:

It is the Hermit good!

He singeth loud his godly hymns

That he makes in the wood.

He'll shrieve my soul, he'll wash away

The Albatross's blood.

大船沉没,拉起漩涡,小船也圈圈打转

第七部分

PART SEVEN

这隐士大德深居林中，　　　　　　　　　　林中隐士，
林子随坡斜向海滩。
那美妙的歌声多么洪亮！
每当有船从异乡返航，
他总爱和水手们畅谈。

THIS Hermit good lives in that wood　　　The Hermit of the Wood,
Which slopes down to the sea.
How loudly his sweet voice he rears!
He loves to talk with marineres
That come from a far countree.

早晚、午时,他一日三祷——
他有一张饱满的跪垫,
一截朽烂的老橡残桩
盖满了厚厚的青苔。

小船靠近,话声传来:
"嘿,这真是怪了!
那一大片的信号灯呢?
刚才还明晃晃的。"

He kneels at morn, and noon, and eve—
He hath a cushion plump:
It is the moss that wholly hides
The rotted old oak-stump.

The skiff-boat neared: I heard them talk,
'Why, this is strange, I trow!
Where are those lights so many and fair,
That signal made but now?'

隐士也说,"确实奇怪!——
喊了也没人应声!
船板七扭八弯!再看船帆,
破破烂烂,薄薄一层!
我从没见过这样的帆篷,
真像那死气沉沉,

骸骨一般,粘着林间溪流
渐漂渐远的黄叶,
在那常春藤上白雪满当,
树上的幼鸮向食崽的恶狼
呼吼连连的时节。"

满怀惊奇地靠近大船。

'Strange, by my faith!' the Hermit said—
'And they answered not our cheer!
The planks looked warped! and see those sails,
How thin they are and sere!
I never saw aught like to them,
Unless perchance it were

Brown skeletons of leaves that lag
My forest-brook along;
When the ivy-tod is heavy with snow,
And the owlet whoops to the wolf below,
That eats the she-wolf's young.'

Approacheth the ship with wonder.

"上帝啊！真是活见鬼了——
（领港人出声应答）
我怕"——可隐士却轻轻松松，
说着"快划，快划！"

小船继续向大船靠拢，
可我没动，也没开腔。
小船刚刚到大船底下，
便传来了隆隆声响。

'Dear Lord! it hath a fiendish look—
(The Pilot made reply)
I am a-feared'—'Push on, push on!'
Said the Hermit cheerily.

The boat came closer to the ship,
But I nor spake nor stirred;
The boat came close beneath the ship,
And straight a sound was heard.

第七部分 / PART SEVEN

它来自水下,越来越大,
越来越叫人害怕。
它劈开海湾,撞向大船,
船像铅一样沉下。 　　　　　　　　　　船突然沉没。

那巨响骇骇,摇天动海,
震得我头昏眼迷。
我漂在海上,像是一块
泡了七天的尸体。
可快如幻梦一场,一觉醒来,
我已在领港人的船里。 　　　　　　　老水手被救上领港人的小船。

Under the water it rumbled on,
Still louder and more dread:
It reached the ship, it split the bay;
The ship went down like lead. 　　　　　The ship suddenly sinketh.

Stunned by that loud and dreadful sound,
Which sky and ocean smote,
Like one that hath been seven days drowned
My body lay afloat;
But swift as dreams, myself I found
Within the Pilot's boat. 　　　　　　　The ancient Mariner is saved
　　　　　　　　　　　　　　　　　　in the Pilot's boat.

大船沉没,拉起漩涡,
小船也圈圈打转。
万物沉静,像在倾听
那独自回响的远山。

我动动嘴唇——那领港人
便哇的一声吓倒在地。
那圣洁的隐士坐地抬眼,
嘴里念起祷词。

Upon the whirl, where sank the ship,
The boat spun round and round;
And all was still, save that the hill
Was telling of the sound.

I moved my lips — the Pilot shrieked
And fell down in a fit;
The holy Hermit raised his eyes,
And prayed where he did sit.

我一拿起桨来,那小孩
便忽然神智大乱。
他放声大笑,笑个没完,
眼珠子来回溜转。
"哈哈!"他说,"我没看错,
魔鬼也会划船。"

终于,我又回到家乡,
踏上坚实的故土!
隐士从船里晃上岸头,
拖着蹒跚的脚步。

I took the oars: the Pilot's boy,
Who now doth crazy go,
Laughed loud and long, and all the while
His eyes went to and fro.
'Ha! ha!' quoth he, 'full plain I see,
The Devil knows how to row.'

And now, all in my own countree,
I stood on the firm land!
The Hermit stepped forth from the boat,
And scarcely he could stand.

"宽恕我吧,圣者大德!"
他在额间划出十字。
"来吧,"他说,"快告诉我——
你究竟是何等人士?"

这一身朽骨痛苦难当,
突然被死死拧住。
它逼我开口,把往事讲述,
不讲便不得舒服。

> 老水手真诚地向隐士恳求宽恕。一生之罚降下。

'O shrieve me, shrieve me, holy man!'
The Hermit crossed his brow.
'Say quick,' quoth he, 'I bid thee say—
What manner of man art thou?'

Forthwith this frame of mine was wrenched
With a woful agony,
Which forced me to begin my tale;
And then it left me free.

> The ancient Mariner earnestly entreateth the Hermit to shrieve him; and the penance of life falls on him.

此后，那痛苦去了又来，
不定在哪个时候。
这吓人的故事从头讲完，
我心头的烈火方休。

我像夜晚一样四处流浪，
我的言语有奇怪的力量，
在遇见某人的那一刹那，
我便知道他要听我说话，
他就是我讲述的对象。

> 终其余生，他都将在不时袭来的剧痛的迫使下四处流浪。

Since then, at an uncertain hour,
That agony returns:
And till my ghastly tale is told,
This heart within me burns.

I pass, like night, from land to land;
I have strange power of speech;
That moment that his face I see,
I know the man that must hear me:
To him my tale I teach.

> And ever and anon throughout his future life an agony constraineth him to travel from land to land;

那门里的喧闹阵阵起爆!

客人们齐声欢笑。

花园凉亭,新娘伴娘

同唱一支小调。

听,那钟声清脆悠扬,

晚祷的时辰已到!

赴宴的客人!这灵魂

曾独自面对淼淼海波。

那样荒凉,那样寂寞,

好像上帝都不曾来过。

What loud uproar bursts from that door!

The wedding-guests are there:

But in the garden-bower the bride

And bride-maids singing are:

And hark the little vesper bell,

Which biddeth me to prayer!

O Wedding-Guest! this soul hath been

Alone on a wide wide sea:

So lonely 'twas, that God himself

Scarce seemèd there to be.

喔，那婚礼盛宴再是甜美，

也远远不及

大家一起往教堂走去，

相伴相随的滋味——

大家一起往教堂走去，

一起诚心祷告。

老人、小孩、亲朋佳侣

和喜笑颜开的少男少女，

人人向圣父弯腰！

O sweeter than the marriage-feast.

'Tis sweeter far to me,

To walk together to the kirk

With a goodly company!—

To walk together to the kirk,

And all together pray,

While each to his great Father bends,

Old men, and babes, and loving friends

And youths and maidens gay!

再见,再见!赴宴的客人,

听我一句忠告!

爱人、也爱鸟兽的人们

才不白白祷告。

对大小生灵爱得越真,

祷告就越有成效。

上帝爱护一切,爱护我们,

一切都由他创造。

老水手以亲身经历教导人们敬爱上帝创造和爱护的一切。

Farewell, farewell! but this I tell
To thee, thou Wedding-Guest!
He prayeth well, who loveth well
Both man and bird and beast.

He prayeth best, who loveth best
All things both great and small;
For the dear God who loveth us,
He made and loveth all.

And to teach, by his own example, love and reverence to all things that God made and loveth.

亮着眼睛，白着胡须，
水手就此走远。
客人也从门口转身，
离开新郎的宅院。

他像挨了当头一棒，丢了
知觉，惘然无神。
第二天清晨，他变得更有
智慧，也更加悲沉。

The Mariner, whose eye is bright,
Whose beard with age is hoar,
Is gone: and now the Wedding-Guest
Turned from the bridegroom's door.

He went like one that hath been stunned,
And is of sense forlorn:
A sadder and a wiser man,
He rose the morrow morn.

夜的抒情歌谣
—— 译后散记

  夜。出酒店醒酒，城河吐着腥膻，挟一汪炙闷闯来，被跟前一条小道拦在光外，拦在音乐之外。婚礼在背后延续，像被捂住了嘴，懵在时光里。点一根烟，歌声溢出礼堂，愣愣传到耳边：

No I've never seen anything quite like you tonight.

  天像只空碗，高高的穹顶。河边一棵梧桐，乍看像片焦黑的肺叶，过滤着光，掩着树下一个偷钓的人，人影孤作一团，不动，没有寡意，守着浮标一颤黄绿，河水哑哑流着：

> 宫殿穹顶投下的阴影
> 随浪起伏，轻漂河腹。
> 泉流与洞穴合鸣，
> 鸣响和谐的旋律。
>
> （——柯勒律治《忽必烈汗》）

  一阵风起，拉动一响震耳的船鸣。肺叶晃出一脸狞笑，又是一响船鸣。两腿怯了似的一软，又是一响，两响：

> 鳄鱼可怕的咆哮，犹如沉重而遥远的雷鸣，不仅摇风动水，亦让大地颤抖——而且，当成千上万条鳄鱼同时纵声而哮，你简直不得不信，整个地球都已不掩凶狂，不罢躁动……
>
> （——柯勒律治出旅美洲荒野时所作笔记）

潮热尽往身上一粘，挤出一股晕眩。紧眼，余光扯开夜幕一角，竟收得一瞬幻景：

> 红日落海，群星奔涌，
> 　暗夜霎时降临。
> 鬼船疾疾驶去，海上
> 　传来遥遥低吟。
>
> （——《古舟子咏》）

睁眼，敞亮的黑暗，船鸣早已消散，河边的人影较劲般暗着，河面五光十色：

> 千千万万黏滑的生物
> 　存活如故……
>
> （——《古舟子咏》）

却已

> ……色彩斑斓：
> 青蓝、油绿，柔绒般黑滑，
> 每一条都尽情舒卷，留下
> 　金色的火光一闪。
>
> （——《古舟子咏》）

婚礼仍在延续，远远地延续，远在一七九七年秋。英伦，湖畔，新人有三：威廉·华兹华斯、多萝西·华兹华斯、塞缪尔·泰勒·柯勒律治。信天翁从极地飞来，见证，留下，被浪漫的弩箭射杀：

想法就这么冒出来了（我不记得是谁想到的）：可以写一系列诗，分两种类型。一类诗里，事件和人、物将至少在某种程度上是超现实的。这类诗歌企望达成的最高目标便是：假定这些情境真实，让自然随之涌现的情绪以其富于戏剧性的真实意义让诗歌的情感获得摄人心魄的魅力。在这个意义上，对任何一个——无论在什么时候，无论是出于何种错觉——曾相信自己受到了超自然力量影响的人来说，这些情境都很真实。而另一类诗，则由日常生活来提供题材；……创作《抒情歌谣》的计划即源于此。计划中，我们商定，我将努力塑造超现实或者至少有其浪漫色彩的人与角色，同时从内在天性中调动一份人性的关注和某种真实的假象，来确保这些想象的影子能在构成"诗性信念"的那一瞬间获得那份心甘情愿的"怀疑暂停"。……抱着这样的态度，我写下了《古舟子咏》。[1]

（——《文学传记》）

浮标晃得像个借口，人影如秘密，肺叶沙沙，又是四声船鸣，像猫头鹰的远祷——四声重音，韵律在实验，是夜的民谣[2]：

嘟——喂！嘟——呜！
它啼罢一声，又接一声，听！
它叫的多么迷糊。

Tu[3]-whit! — Tu-whoo!
And hark, again! the crowing cock,
How drowsily it crew.

（——柯勒律治《克里斯塔贝尔》）

船去，那浮标暗下，光弱得像被扼住了咽喉：

我朋友的诗确有重大缺陷；第一，首要人物没有鲜明的性格，既不见水手的内行，亦无一个长期处于超自然作用的控制之下的人所应享有的某种超自然性；第二，他并不作用，而是持续受到作用；第三，没有必然关联的事件并不互为因果；最后，意象的积累有些太过造作。……[4]

（——1800年版《抒情歌谣》）

忽然，一星光灭，人影泄劲儿似的一松：

诗歌已经毫无可能。一切尝试都将把我赶入那个充斥着尖锐情感的领域……

（——笔记）

片刻，那光点重新亮起，像想起了什么：

——一出诗人幻想[5]

（——1800年版《抒情歌谣》中《古舟子咏》的副标题）

片刻间，那人影像去了哪里，匆匆往返，带回天顶一轮锐利的新月，喘了几下，又从容定下新的形体，雕塑般凝着。一只水鸟魂灵般掠过，嗖地刮着越发浓黑的肺叶，扎进空中，披上浅白的月帘，复活，是信天翁，飞还极地冰寒：

陷入奇异神迷的格陵兰巫师
穿透覆于深渊之上、人迹未至的
重重洋床之域，直至那个位于深渊顶端，
被殊形骇状，绝非大地、空气抑或
渊上之海孕育的奇观异景围绕的洞穴：

洞中住着狂怒之形，无眠的寂静守卫着
它无人知晓的名字，充满渴望的眼睛，
苍白的脸颊，悬停的呼吸和因惧怕声响
而半张的双唇；……
终在凶残的海之守吏的愤然追逐下，
伴着遥遥可闻的喘息，赶在冰霜
封冻归门之前，再度占据他那
血肉筑成，已为一族畏怯之众
在那无人借居的暗帐中逗留良久的
寓宅。——狂野的幻想！……[6]

（——《民族的命运》）

回神，雨已识趣地下了几分。浮标、人影，都糊在湿淋淋的灰里。月摁住水雾，迎着肺叶张牙舞爪的责难：

一颗明星被月尖勾起，
在月弯里闪烁。

（——《古舟子咏》）

——像不可抗拒的叮咛：

In the touch of this bosom there worketh a spell
Which is lord of thy utterance, Christabel!

我这胸脯的触碰将唤醒一种魔力，
它就是你言语的主宰，克里斯塔贝尔！

（——《克里斯塔贝尔》）

你会

…pass, like night, from land to land;

……像夜晚一样四处流浪；

（——《古舟子咏》）

你的言语

……have strange power……

……有奇怪的力量；

（——《古舟子咏》）

——一个男孩气鼓鼓跑出酒店，甩着哭腔，径直朝暗里奔去，像极了两个世纪前的那个夜晚，老柯勒律治家的幺子对恶兄挺刀相向，被始终站在兄长们一边的母亲缴械，后夺门而逃，不愿回家，在奥特尔河边藏了一宿、睡了一宿，熬过

一个可怕的风雨之夜。

（——笔记）

但等待他的，不是

此后多年……始终虚弱，饱受寒热之苦。

（——笔记）

也不是鸦片成瘾的肺叶，不是孤独的背影，也不是那浮标般挥之不去的

……耻辱的标志，悲伤的印记。
（——《克里斯塔贝尔》）

等待他的，只是一个温柔的夜。歌声仍在循环，却不再是

No I've never seen anything quite like you tonight.

而是抒情歌谣的回声——

No I've never seen anything
quite like you tonight.

叶紫

2022 年 6 月 27 日

于南京

译后记小注

1 序言中提及的"明确声明"即为此段。
2 柯勒律治在其三大"梦幻之诗"（即《忽必烈汗》《古舟子咏》和《克里斯塔贝尔》）的创作过程中，无时不需要鸦片的慰藉（因少时受过严重风寒，落下一生不除的病根），无时不需要华兹华斯的友情（一场短暂的"婚姻"，终于华兹华斯对《古舟子咏》的苛评），也无时不践行着独特的韵律（在很长一段时间里，和《古舟子咏》的"道德问题"一样，柯式"新韵律"同样受到了"韵律正统"的严酷指摘）。柯勒律治的"新韵律"是对传统民谣韵律的回归与发展，亦强调"只计重音数量，不计音节多少（和严格抑扬）"。《古舟子咏》大体上处于"四重—三重"和"四重—四重—三重"模式组成的节奏之中，如：

> Her lips were red, her looks were free,（四重抑扬）
> Her locks were yellow as gold:（三重抑扬）
> Her skin was as white as leprosy,（四重抑扬）
> The Nightmare Life-In-Death was she,（四重抑扬）
> Who thicks man's blood with cold.（三重抑扬）

> 她唇色 / 红艳 /，神情 / 放纵 /，
> 金发 / 熠熠 / 满头 /。
> 她肤色 / 惨白 /，如害 / 麻风 /，
> 她是名叫 / "死中 / 之生" / 的恶梦 /，
> 能以冰寒 / 冻人 / 血流 /。

在大部分诗行遵循严谨的抑扬节奏（大体上即指"轻重相间"的节奏）的情况下，柯勒律治时而放弃严格的抑扬，让重音和重音连续出现，营建独特的"反正统音效"（即古老民谣中常见的"跳韵"），如：

> I pass, like night, from land to land;（四重抑扬）
> I have strange power of speech;（三重非抑扬，连续重音）
> That moment that his face I see,（四重非抑扬，连续重音）
> I know the man that must hear me:（四重非抑扬，连续重音）
> To him my tale I teach.（三重抑扬）

> 我像夜晚 / 一样 / 四处 / 流浪 /，
> 我的言语 / 有奇怪的 / 力量 /，
> 在我遇见 / 某人的 / 那一 / 刹那 /，
> 我便知道 / 他要 / 听我 / 说话 /，
> 他就是 / 我讲述 / 的对象 /。

这一版《古舟子咏》译文尽可能还原了原作的韵律模式，旨在让读者更明确地感受到柯式韵律的神妙。有时，因为中英文的差异，更有待读者根据韵律模式，发挥想象，做出"音乐诠释"，完成符合原诗节奏的朗读，如：

Slowly the sounds came back again,
Now mixed, now one by one.

接着 /,又缓缓 / 落回 / 海上 /,
时而独唱 /,时而 / 和响 /。

读者可以将以上诗文中可能因为节奏惯性落在第一个"时而"上的重音压住,让声音平顺地划过,让第一声重音落在"独唱"上,和自然落在第二个"时而"与"合响"上的重音构成"三重"。
3 以下划波浪线标出者均为重读音节,后同。
4 序言中提及的"被华兹华斯一丝不苟地上了编号的四个'重大缺陷'"即为此段。
5 "一出诗人幻想"这个副标题,在我个人看来,也是一种看似妥协的保护:表面上在"道德问题"上向"巴勃尔德夫人们"妥协,实际上在保护柯式新韵律。
6 参照《古舟子咏》中的

……
我们闯入那片无人涉足、
没有声息的海洋。

以及

……
她肤色惨白,如害麻风,
她是名叫"死中之生"的噩梦,
……